W9-BIO-844

To: Michaela,

Hugs & Kisses

Grandma

Uncle Giorgio

Marie-Aude Murail was born in Havre, France, in 1954. At a young age she knew she loved writing. She studied liberal arts and received her doctorate. Married, mother of two boys, she now writes stories for children. Her books have been published by Centurion, Gallimard, Nathan and École des Loisirs.

Yves Besnier was born in Angers, France, in 1954, and studied fine arts. After finishing his studies, he began illustrating posters, books (published by Gallimard, Nathan, Hatier and Centurion), and children's magazines. Nowadays, he paints most of the time; but in his spare time, he writes children's stories under the pseudonym of Igor Gonzola.

Library of Congress Cataloging-in-Publication Data
available upon request
ISBN 0-89565-809-7

Uncle Giorgio

A story written by Marie-Aude Murail
illustrated by Yves Besnier

THE CHILD'S WORLD
MANKATO, MINNESOTA

A funny allergy

Mr. Giorgio has an embarrassing disease:
little boys give him a rash and little girls
make him sneeze. He is allergic to children.
When he sees a little boy on the street, he

itches between his fingers or has to scratch his neck. The next thing he knows - he has a rash.

No matter how far away a little girl is, Mr. Giorgio knows she's coming because his nose starts to run.

"Achoo!"

If too many little girls go by him, poor Mr. Giorgio needs to blow his nose.

Because of this allergy, Mr. Giorgio never goes for a walk when school is out and he avoids going to the parks. He bought a secluded house surrounded by a garden and he put up a sign, "Beware of Dog." Even though he doesn't have a dog, he knows children are afraid of mean dogs.

Because of his allergy, Mr. Giorgio choses his friends carefully. He prefers grumpy bachelors who haven't the slightest idea of getting married or having children.

But from time to time one of his bachelor friends will end up getting married! Mr. Giorgio will take several evenings to explain to the newlyweds all the problems, troubles, and catastrophes that come from having children.

"They always get the measles," he says.

"They come down with a fever whenever you want to go to the movies. They get holes in their pants as soon as you buy them. And on their birthdays, they stuff themselves so much that they are sick that whole night long."

"Ha! ha! crazy Giorgio," say his friends slapping him on the back. "What a kidder! Always a funny line!"

In short, as far as Mr. Giorgio is concerned, there are too many children in the streets, too many bachelors getting married and everything is going downhill.

Two germs arrive

One day while Mr. Giorgio was eating breakfast in his kitchen, he almost choked on his toast.

In his hand he held a letter from his brother Peppo who lives three hundred miles away. The letter read, "My dear

brother, My wife has been in the hospital since yesterday, because in a month she's having a baby and she's supposed to take it easy. And I'm leaving Sunday for Venezuela. My wife was crying this morning she was so upset and she asked me who could take care of the children. I immediately said to her, "My dear, dry your eyes. What about Giorgio! The children will love staying with him - he is such a funny guy!

I'm sending the children on the train Sunday morning. I know that you will be happy to have them with you. I have already notified the school in your neighborhood and the principal said they would be glad to have Federico and Juiletta, your dear nephew and niece, for a month.

A big hug from all of us,
Your brother Peppo."

Still coughing from the toast, Mr. Giorgio read and reread the letter. He said quietly, "This is a nightmare."

He pinched his arms and rubbed his eyes. But it did no good. It didn't change a single word in the letter.

For the next week, Mr. Giorgio was up to strange things in his house. He dragged

mattresses up to the attic and down to the cellar. He fixed up a pulley on the roof. He went to a music shop and bought a bugle. Then he went to an art shop and came back with a can of white paint. Once he had everything ready, Mr. Giorgio calmed down a little.

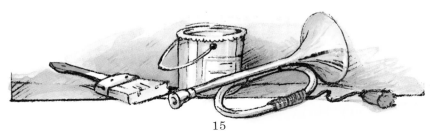

Federico and Juiletta

Sunday evening, Giorgio put on sunglasses so he couldn't see little Federico, he held a handkerchief over his nose so he couldn't smell Juiletta and, dragging his

16

heels, he went to the train station.

When the train stopped, two children jumped off the train. Federico is a good-looking nine-year-old boy, with dark eyes, and brown curly hair. His sister, Juiletta, is a lovely six-year old with sky-blue eyes and golden hair.

"How horrible!" groaned Uncle Giorgio when he saw the darling children from

under his sunglasses.

"Hello, Uncle!" the children said. "Are you all right? You're wearing such funny glasses! Do you have a cold? When are we going? Why are you scratching? Why do you have a rash on your nose?"

"And blah-blah-blah," muttered Uncle Giorgio, "Did they give you parakeet feed, or what?"

The two children burst out laughing because they had been told what a kidder

their uncle Giorgio was.

When they got to their uncle's house, he waved them in, "Don't stay in the living room, I can't stand the smell of little girls!"

Juiletta and Federico screamed with laughter. What a good time they will have at Uncle Giorgio's!

"Come with me," he said, "I'll show you your room. And you are not to leave it! I can't stand to look at little boys!"

No, it's too much, too funny! Federico

was in tears from laughing so hard.

Uncle Giorgio took them up two flights of stairs. Then he leaned a ladder against the wall and, once at the top of the ladder, he pushed open a trap door.

"The attic!" exclaims Juiletta. "This is our room?"

"Yes, and I'm sleeping in the cellar," says Uncle Giorgio.

Sleeping in the attic, on mattresses on the floor, in the middle of a pile of junk, what great fun for the children!

"Oh, thanks, Uncle!" said Federico.

But Uncle Giorgio had already closed the trap door behind him and, holding his nose, he descended to the cellar, his new bedroom.

A witch's house

"Me, I'm sleeping right here," said Juiletta, stretching out on a mattress.

Her brother glanced around with a puzzled look.

"What's the matter with you?" asked his sister.

"Aren't you hungry?"

"Yeah, but Uncle is surely going to call us for dinner."

"You think so?"

Federico was not so sure. Standing next to his bed, he saw a sheet of paper on his pillow. It was a note from Uncle Giorgio that said simply, "To eat, open the window."

"It's a witch's house," murmured his sister.

Federico was too hungry to be afraid. He opened the window, but then he jumped back and gave a little shriek. He saw a large basket floating in the air. He went back to look at it and lifted his head up: the basket was attached to a hook, the hook was tied to a rope, the rope went up to a pulley and then back down to the ground. Juiletta clapped her hands, "Fantastic! It's like being in a grand castle."

"No, more like being on a ocean liner."

The two children lifted down the basket and while eating pizza, cheese, and grapes, invented all sorts of stories. Then, exhausted, they went to bed with their clothes on.

"Do you think Uncle Giorgio is going to come up and wake us up for school?" mumbled Federico who was already

dreaming.

"Sure," answered Juiletta, yawning.

The next morning, Federico was busy dreaming that he had joined the army, when he woke up with a start. Strange music was wafting up from the garden. Federico ran to the window and down below saw his Uncle Giorgio playing a military march on the bugle.

"Is it time to go to school?" yelled Federico. "Yes," answered Uncle Giorgio. "The way to school is easy: I marked it with white arrows on the sidewalk. Bye-bye!"

"Uncle Giorgio was in a hurry!" said Federico, closing the window. "Do you think he made us breakfast?"

"Of course! He is so nice!" Juiletta exclaimed. "He even invented a game for us to get to school!"

The children went down to the kitchen and found two bowls on the table.

"But the milk is cold!" reported Federico, upset.

"All we have to do is heat it up," replied

Juiletta, giving the matches to her older brother.

Federico was not allowed to light matches at home. But, at Uncle Giorgio's, he could do anything! While Federico struck the matches, Juiletta cut some odd-shaped pieces of bread, very thick at one end and then skinny at the other. You should know that at home, Juiletta wasn't allowed to use the knife.

"Should we make toast?"

"Good idea! Yikes, watch out for the milk!"

Too late, the milk had boiled over.

"There's some left," Federico said hopefully. "Yikes, watch out. The toast..."

The pieces of bread were too big. They got stuck in the toaster and it started to smoke. Finally, the two children sat at the table eating their burnt pieces of toast with their scorched milk.

"Yum, what a feast!"

"And we made it all ourselves!"

After breakfast, they picked up their backpacks. They could hardly wait to follow the arrows that Uncle Giorgio had painted for them.

Off to school!

Once they started off, Federico began to worry, "Do you think we'll find the school?"
"Sure! Uncle Giorgio loves us too much to let us get lost. See, there's an arrow!"

Every few steps, on the sidewalk and
even on the street, Uncle Giorgio had
painted clear white arrows. Finally, the
children came in view of the school. The
other students gathered around them, "The

new kids!"

Federico and Juiletta were a little intimidated. They were asked their names, how old they were. The other children touched their clothes, kicked their backpacks. Then they were asked where they lived.

"With Uncle Giorgio," said Federico.

"What is he like?" asked Steven

The children were happy to tell them everything that had happened since they

got to Uncle Giorgio's.

"What? Your room is the attic?" Ellen said, surprised.

"Your dinner comes in a basket?" repeated Albert.

"You get to sleep with your clothes on?" Carl asked enviously.

But one of the older kids, Paul, shrugged his shoulders, "Yeah, sure, what do you think we are - stupid?"

The teacher who heard everything came up and yelled at Federico, "Are you finished with your tall tale? Go get in line."

This made Federico angry and during recess, he got in a fight with Paul, and got a nice black eye.

"Do you think that Uncle Giorgio remembered a snack for us?" he asked his sister when they left school.

"Of course!"

But no, there wasn't a thing on the table in the kitchen.

"I know, we can make a cake with eggs and apples!"

As soon as it was said, it was done. The cake was delicious, a little less burned than the toast. Just then Uncle Giorgio came home from the office. He came into the kitchen with his umbrella opened in front of him like a shield.

"Leave," he yelled, "get out of here! Up to the attic!"

It was so cool to have an uncle who liked to play. Federico let out a war cry. He took a wooden spoon and a lid and pretended he was fencing, "He's mine, gallant knights! Kill the traitor!"

The big party

The next day at school, all the kids gathered around the newcomers again and asked them questions. In their hearts, they all wanted to believe in Uncle Giorgio, even Paul.

Federico generously invited them all over. "You all can come to our uncle's on Saturday and you'll see - he will play with us!"

On Saturday, all the school children came running in together to Uncle Giorgio's garden. When he saw them coming, he turned and ran as fast as he could.

"Wow!" shouted Paul, "We're playing tag, he's it. This way!"

"No, this way!"
screamed Steven.
You've never seen
an adult run as fast
as Uncle Giorgio
did that Saturday.

Carl found him
in the attic and
suddenly he was in
the cellar. Ellen
saw him hidden
under the kitchen
table, and two seconds
later, Albert discovered
him in the dog house.

All afternoon, the children tried to catch Uncle Giorgio.

How they laughed, especially when Uncle Giorgio crawled into the basket hanging from the pulley.

"What a card your Uncle Giorgio is!" said Paul.

Federico and Juiletta were very

proud of their uncle. He had become a real celebrity in the neighborhood. Now, all the children happily waved to him, "Good day, Giorgio!" they said when he ventured out, creeping along close to the walls.

So, at the end of a month, Federico and Juiletta were sad to have to leave their uncle Giorgio! However, they were glad to be going home to Mom and Dad.

Giorgio and Georgette

Poor Mr. Giorgio took a whole week of vacation off after the children left. He was covered with a rash and his nose wouldn't stop running. Finally, on Saturday, he

felt a bit better. Then he got another letter. The letter was from Federico and Juiletta's mom:

Dear Uncle Giorgio,
I'm writing to tell you the good news!
Several days ago, I became the proud mother
of twins, named Giorgio and Georgette,
after you. Oh, dear uncle, how can I thank
you for all you've done for our children? I
almost didn't recognize them, they have
changed so much. Federico, who has always
been a worrier, is much more sure of himself.

A real little man! I used to be afraid even to let him light matches. And Juiletta has changed too. She is as helpful as a princess. Right now, she gets dressed by herself, she makes her own toast.

Dear Uncle Giorgio, thanks a million! If the twins could talk, do you know what they'd say? They would say, "When do we get to go to Uncle Giorgio's, like Federico and Juiletta?"